WHEN I KILL YOU

MICHELLE WAN

RAVE[N]
an i[...]
ORCA BOO[...]

Library and Archives Canada Cataloguing in Publication

Wan, Michelle
When I kill you / Michelle Wan.
(Rapid reads)

Issued also in electronic formats.
ISBN 978-1-55469-990-2

I. Title. II. Series: Rapid reads
PS8645.A53W54 2012 C813'.6 C2011-907746-9

First published in the United States, 2012
Library of Congress Control Number: 2011943705

Summary: When mud-wrestling postal worker Gina Lopez is blackmailed, the results are amusing, confusing and potentially life-threatening as she strives to find ways not to carry out a contract killing. (RL 3.8)

Orca Book Publishers is dedicated to preserving the environment and has printed this book on paper certified by the Forest Stewardship Council®.

Orca Book Publishers gratefully acknowledges the support for its publishing programs provided by the following agencies: the Government of Canada through the Canada Book Fund and the Canada Council for the Arts, and the Province of British Columbia through the BC Arts Council and the Book Publishing Tax Credit.

Design by Teresa Bubela
Cover photography by iStockphoto.com

ORCA BOOK PUBLISHERS
PO Box 5626, Stn. B
Victoria, BC Canada
V8R 6S4

ORCA BOOK PUBLISHERS
PO Box 468
Custer, WA USA
98240-0468

www.orcabook.com
Printed and bound in Canada.

15 14 13 12 • 4 3 2 1

To Frances Hanna

CHAPTER ONE

I was jogging lightly in place at ringside while Al, the owner of Al's Roadhouse & Pit, worked up the crowd.

"Our own luscious Lady Lava," he yelled, pointing at me. "A homegrown talent, five feet seven, one hundred and thirty pounds of dynamite. And does this lady love mud!"

I pumped my arms. The crowd, mostly men, whistled and cheered. Jimmy came out from the bar to give me a high five. He was the bartender at Al's and my main supporter.

"Good luck, kid," he shouted over the noise.

"And weighing in at a hundred and forty-five, five feet eight of sheer swamp instinct, from Sarnia, Ontario...Wild... Woman...Wanda!"

More cheers. Wanda muscled forward and performed a little jig.

There was a big crowd out, a hundred at least. Most of the spectators were locals from the town and surrounding area. There wasn't a lot to do in Franks, Ontario, on a hot Sunday night in August. But they came from all over. Windsor, London, Hamilton, Toronto, some from as far away as Sudbury. Most of the guys had never seen female mud wrestling. Most of them were there for the skin. They wanted to ogle two semi-nude girls scrambling around getting dirty. They wanted a bit of titillation and a lot of laughs. A few, like me, took it seriously. I wore a one-piece suit, not a bikini. I'd been district girls' wrestling champ in high school, and I knew the moves. So did Wanda. That was what made her such a tough opponent. That and the fact that she'd do anything to win.

While Al gabbed on about the future of mud wrestling in Canada, which was happening *here*, thanks to him, we climbed into the ring. The ring was outside behind the roadhouse. It was six feet square and the bottom was covered in mud. It should have been good quality bentonite, the kind of stuff they used in spas, but Al was cheap. It was the coarse stuff mixed with other junk to cut the cost. On the other hand, give the devil his due, Al's was one of the few places, other than one-off events, where you could see real mud wrestling. The sport had never taken off here the way it did south of the border. Too cold most of the year.

I was now kneeling in my corner, glaring across at Wanda, who was kneeling in hers and glaring back. I wanted to show her

I wasn't afraid of her, even though I knew she was big, mean and popular. I'd only met her once before. She beat me more by acclaim than on points, because the rules of wrestling are pretty loosely applied. Who wins is often who the crowd cheers loudest for. Or throws the most money at. That's something Al does his best to encourage.

We both went through the routine of the mud bath. The first few seconds can be critical in mud wrestling. Smearing yourself with mud straight off makes you slippery and harder to grab.

"Okay, ladies," Al mouthed into the mike. "This is a three-round match. You know the rules. No biting, scratching or hairpulling. You must remain in the mud at all times. You may not rise beyond a kneeling position. And no pulling off each other's clothing." Boos from the crowd.

"Are you ready?" He did the countdown. "Mud wrestle!"

Wanda came out of her corner fast, but I was faster. In mud wrestling it's speed, not size, that matters. I was on her and we grappled for a few seconds, shoving and sliding. I broke and came back to grapple again. This time I made a neat pass behind her and locked one arm around her neck. I tried to slide the other under her knee in a quick cradle that would tie her up like a package, but she bucked and managed to break my hold. This is where mud really adds another dimension to wrestling. It's slippery and unpredictable.

Now we were shoulder to shoulder, pushing and scrambling on our knees. Her weight gave her an advantage. I found myself giving ground bit by bit as she bulldozed me back. One of her well-known ploys was to throw her opponent right out of the mud. It was a real crowd pleaser and usually ended the match. She had me jammed up against the foam wall of the ring now, and the crowd was chanting, "Go! Go! Go!"

I sensed her tensing for the big push. I let her think she had me. Just as she drove in for the final ram, I managed to twist aside. It was enough to skew her balance. I followed up like lightning, using her momentum to pitch her on her back. Mud flew. The crowd loved it. Then I was all over her in a full body press. She flailed around to shake me, bridging and bucking. I stuck to her like wet clay, trying to force the pin. But she was strong and her shoulders wouldn't cooperate. The crowd was going nuts. Then the bell clanged to end the round.

"You're crap, Lava," Wanda sneered as we separated.

When the whistle went for Round Two, I launched myself at her, but Wanda was prepared for me. We slapped skin, shoved head-to-head. Suddenly she ducked and grabbed me around the middle. We rolled. I slithered loose. We came at each other again, locking arms. This time I got her in a leg clamp and held her for a few seconds before she wriggled free. Now it was her turn to toss me around. I tried to stabilize, but my knee slid out from under me. Next thing I knew I was facedown in the mud. She really ground me in it.

"Eat dirt," she rasped in my left ear. I hooked my leg around hers, lost the hold, hooked again. Over the shouting I heard Jimmy yelling something at me. I gave a tremendous buck, managed to get my arms and knees under me. She stayed on top of me, but at least I was up for air. My eyes were so caked with mud I could barely see. I was thankful when the bell rang.

We were both breathing hard as we went into Round Three. We slammed together, sort of falling onto each other. More grappling, shoving, circling. Wanda got me in a wristlock, did a quick shift, got behind me and threw a half nelson. She had me for a moment before I wriggled free. We separated and came together again. But I was running out of gas. She sensed it and used it to her advantage to throw me sideways and slam me on my back. Along the way she drove her knee into my stomach—hard. It knocked the wind out of me, and suddenly she was straddling me, heavy as a landslide, going for the pin. I struggled to bridge.

She growled, this time in my right ear, "You're dead meat, Lava," and gave me a quick, sharp head butt that had me blinking stars. Al, who was refereeing, pretended not to see. But I could hear Jimmy in my corner yelling, "Foul!"

The butt stunned me, and that was all Wild Woman Wanda needed. She threw her full weight on me in a press. Al was with us in the ring, bent double, hand out, waiting to signal the pin. I tried to kick free but was too exhausted. My shoulders sagged. Al's hand lowered for the count. One! Two! Three! I was down for the fall.

CHAPTER TWO

I had mud in my eyes. And in my hair and mouth and up my nose. That's the worst of mud wrestling. When you lose, you lose dirty. I staggered around the building to the hose-down pad. The plumbing at Al's is old, and he doesn't want mud clogging up his drains. So the "talent," as he calls us girls, has to hose off outside before we hit the showers. Shower, I should say, because there was only one, and we had to queue for it. Meantime the crowd was going crazy for Wild Woman Wanda. I could see her as I turned the water on. She was pumping her fists over her head and making biceps, posing left and right.

Jimmy appeared as I was rinsing out my mouth.

"Tough break, Lava." He shook his head. Jimmy was a little guy, skinny as a wire, twice my age, twice as wise and a good friend.

"She butted me!"

"I saw."

"I—want—a rematch," I told him between gargles.

"Give it a rest. This is the second time you've lost to Wanda. You're not ready, kid. You gotta get more fit."

"Hey, I jog."

"When you feel like it. And you eat lousy."

"I want the rematch, Jimbo." I was in no mood for lectures. "Next week. I'll swamp that hairpulling hippo."

Right then Al showed up to bawl at Jimmy that folks were lining up for drinks and was he going to take all night?

"Keep your pants on," muttered Jimmy. He hurried away.

By now you know my dimensions and my stage name, Lady Lava. What you don't know is that I'm otherwise Gina Lopez, twenty-six, brown eyes, blond hair that only needs a touch-up now and then. Like Al said, I'm a local girl, born and raised in Franks. A postal worker during the week and a mud wrestler on weekends. Right now I wrestle in Al's pit for the experience, racking up small-time wins and, yeah, the occasional loss. I want to build my name and hit the action south of the border. Vegas is my dream. I certainly don't wrestle for the glory or the money. The purse, as Al calls it, is a lousy fifty bucks a match. He's never short on takers though. You may not believe it, but there are always chicks who think it looks like fun. Or who do it to please their boyfriends. Or to attract a guy. Al is ever ready to oblige. Any female who's willing can wrestle.

"Listen, girls," Al says to us. "I'm a big promoter of the sport, which is why I run the pit. If I was a businessman, I wouldn't do it. I'm not getting rich here."

He's lying, of course. We women pull in the crowd for him. Semi-pros like me and Wanda, and wannabes out to try their luck. He pockets the profit. We get to supply our own shampoo and towels.

There's something else you need to know about me. I'm also a recent widow. I buried my husband Chico exactly thirty days ago. To be honest, I was more down about my loss to Wanda tonight than I was about Chico.

First, because I hate being beaten. Second, I hate being beaten by a dirty fighter like Wanda. Third, Chico wasn't worth grieving over. Not after what he did to me. Or tried to do.

I was just entering the Ladies when someone called my name. I turned. It was a woman, fiftyish, faded hair locked in a hard perm, a discontented face. She was small and kind of doughy. Her flesh bagged around her ankles and her expandable watchband cut into her pudgy wrists. She wore a frilly blouse, a print cotton skirt, canvas flats and carried a straw handbag. She didn't look like one of Al's regulars. In fact, she'd have been more at home at a church picnic.

"Are you Gina Lopez?" Her voice had a hoity-toity lift to it.

"Lady Lava to you," I said. "Look, I'm not signing autographs right now. If you don't mind." I pushed through and headed to the shower.

She followed me in and shut the door behind her. "I don't want your autograph. I want to talk to you."

Oh cripes, I thought. *Not another one who wants to tell me mud wrestling is un-Christian or degrading to women*. I keyed open the locker where my stuff was stowed.

There were two of them—battered metal high school gym rejects—for the wrestlers. The only thing, other than mud and water, Al supplied.

"Can't it wait?" I peeled off my wrestling suit. She looked away, like seeing me in the raw was improper. I stepped into the stall and turned the water on full bore.

But she wasn't going to be put off. She went on talking at me while I showered. I could see her mouth working through the gap in the curtain even though I couldn't hear her. I took my time soaping off and followed with a good long rinse.

"Hand me my towel, will you," I said when I had finished. I pointed to my stuff in the open locker.

She didn't oblige. Instead she got pushy. "I *said*, in case you didn't hear me, I *saw* what you did."

"Well, it wasn't my best performance," I had to admit. I brushed past her to get the towel myself. She jumped back, like getting wet would ruin her clothes.

"I'm not talking about your wrestling," she said. "I'm talking about the tenth of July, Lovers' Leap."

It took a minute or two for her words to sink in. She watched me, like a cat eyeballs a bird. I registered the date and place all right. Despite the hot shower, I suddenly felt a chill. I dried off slowly, pulled on my bra and pants. Was she talking about Chico's death?

"What about it?" I said at last.

"I *saw* you push him off that cliff."

I stared at her, my mouth hanging open. "You *what*? Who the hell *are* you?"

She held her straw handbag in front of her like a shield.

"My name is Marcia Beekland," she said, talking real fast. "And I'm here to tell you I was hiking up on Lovers' Leap that day. I saw you struggling with a man at the edge of the cliff. *I saw you push him over!*"

"You're crazy!" I shook my head and backed away from her. That wasn't how it happened.

She smiled her cat smile.

"I have the proof. I videoed it on my iPhone. I found out who you were from the newspaper. They called it an accident. *A Tragic Anniversary Picnic*. You'd both been drinking. Your husband—Chico—tripped and fell. It was a hundred-foot drop. I made some inquiries. He had a life insurance policy worth two hundred and fifty thousand dollars, didn't he? A pretty good motive for getting rid of him."

"Listen." I moved so fast she barely had time to flinch. I grabbed her shirtfront, jerking her in close. She batted at me with her hands and dropped her purse. "The life-insurance policy was *his* idea, and it was the other way around." I gave her a few shakes just so she'd get my meaning. "Sure, there was a struggle. But what you *think* you saw was actually Chico trying to get rid of *me*. And by the way, the coroner's verdict was accidental death. Plain and simple. Now get out of my face before I wreck you!"

She pulled loose from me and straightened her clothes.

"I doubt that's how the police will view it," she said primly. "Or the insurance company when they see what I have to show them. They'll want their money back."

In fact, North American Life was dragging its feet on paying out. Of course, I wasn't going to tell her that. Or the fact that the cops *had* talked to me. But I had stuck to my story of an accident, and in the end they let it go.

"Get out," I said.

She bent down, retrieved her purse and pulled out her iPhone.

"Maybe this will convince you," she said and held it up.

On the screen I saw a tiny Gina and Chico seesawing on a cliff edge. The scene lasted for only ten seconds or so before Gina gave Chico what certainly looked like a push that sent him over. It was enough for me to realize how things would be interpreted.

I snatched the phone from her and slammed it on the counter. I slammed it again and again until it came apart in little pieces.

She laughed. "You're not stupid enough to think I didn't download this?"

"Are you threatening me?" I said, realizing she was.

She had regained her confidence now.

"Let's just say I'm concerned about your welfare. I'd like you to stay out of jail. I'd like you to collect a quarter of a million dollars."

"And what's in it for you, all this concern for my welfare?"

She smirked.

"A small favor. In return for my silence. You seem pretty good at getting rid of people. I want you to get rid of someone for me."

When I got my breath back, I said, "Are you nuts? You're trying to blackmail me into *killing* someone for you?"

"Let's just say I'm making you an offer you can't refuse. I'll be in the IGA parking lot at nine tomorrow morning. Look for a white Ford Fiesta. We'll talk then. And, Gina, I want you to know, if you don't show, I'll go public. So this is a meeting you don't want to miss." She walked to the door and pulled it open. Over her shoulder she said, "Nine AM sharp. I'll expect you," and walked out.

I stood there, not believing what I'd just heard. Then I put the toilet seat lid down and sat on it and held my head. I could see what it would look like to the cops. And to the insurance company, who would love a reason not to pay up.

I thought, *Chico, you bastard.*

He was a womanizer and a gambler. I knew that when I married him. But he was good-looking, with dark curly hair and coffee-colored eyes and a wild sense of humor. I even thought his taking out a joint life-insurance policy was a wacky joke. I never dreamed he'd try to kill me for it.

The sad thing is, for a while there on July 10, our seventh anniversary, I thought I was having one of the happiest days of my married life. Chico had put together a cooler of smoked salmon and potato salad, a shaker of shooters and a couple of bottles of champagne—the high-class stuff—with proper champagne glasses, not plastic. He'd hiked us up to a secluded spot high up above Winona Gorge. The view was great. He'd even thought to bring a blanket to lie on, cushions, a tape deck with romantic music.

"Here's to you, Gina," he said and kept refilling my glass.

Then he said, "Hey, babe, come look at this." And he took me over to the edge of the cliff.

That's when he tried to give me the push. I thought he was playing around, and I remember saying, "Hey, Chico, stop it, man. It's dangerous." It took me a second to realize he wasn't joking. He should have known better. You don't shove a mud wrestler. I told myself over and over it was a case of self-defense. And it was. Except for that split second, just as he was toppling backward, when *maybe* I could have saved him. I could have lunged forward and grabbed him. Maybe. But I didn't. Let's say I was in shock and fighting for my life. Or that in that moment I realized what a worthless shit I was married to. And it was Chico who took the quick way down.

Suddenly the Ladies room door swung open and Wild Woman Wanda burst in. She was dripping from her hose-down and her bottle-red hair was plastered to her face. A big gal whose trademark was a leopard-skin off-one-shoulder wrestling suit. It made her look like a chunky Tarzan.

"Bad luck, Lava," she crowed as she strutted past me to the shower. She liked me about as much as I liked her. "You need to work on your technique, girl." Wanda coming on top of Marcia Beekland was more than I could handle.

"Try me for a rematch, mud skipper," I yelled. *"I'll murder you!"* Then I realized what I had said.

CHAPTER THREE

I didn't sleep at all that night. I closed my eyes, but those ten seconds on the cliff kept replaying in my mind. The video was damning. There was no way the cops would accept a claim of self-defense, no way North American Life would cut a check. But I needed the money. A loan shark named Bernie, a gorilla with a broken nose, was hounding me for thirty thousand bucks, Chico's gambling debts. He was being patient while I waited for the insurance payout. But any day now I expected him to get nasty. I had to keep that date with Marcia.

I dragged myself up at daybreak Monday morning, grabbed my iPod and went for a run. I hoped it would clear my head. It didn't. After I got back, I showered. I gulped a cup of coffee, strong and black. Normally I take it sweet with cream with a donut on the side. I ate some dry toast. I almost heaved it up. At 8:00 I called my boss at the post office to say I'd be late for work.

"What is it this time?" Roz said.

I'd already had quite a bit of time off because of Chico, and she was running out of sympathy and tired of having to find someone to cover for me. I could have said quite honestly, "I'm in a fix. I'm being blackmailed and I'm going to have to kill someone, so it's not looking like a good day here." Instead, I said, "Emergency dental appointment. I—ah—broke a tooth."

"Which tooth?"

I wasn't prepared for that. "Um, back incisor."

"You mean front, don't you? Incisors are at the front."

"Oh, yeah," I lied. "Sorry. It really hurts and I'm not thinking straight. I was lucky to get this appointment. I'll be in as soon as I can."

"Do that," Roz snapped.

For once I chose my clothes with care. I needed to look like someone Marcia couldn't haul around, even if she had me pinned. I decided on all black—black T-shirt, black slacks, black leather belt. No accessories.

At five minutes to nine I nudged my old blue Honda into the supermarket parking lot. It was almost empty so it was easy for me to pick out Marcia's car. She was sitting in it, wearing sunglasses. I rolled into the spot next to her. But she didn't want to talk there. She started up her motor and signaled for me to follow her.

She pulled out, turning right on Ebert. She led me straight through town. Soon we were out in the country with nothing but farmland all around us. As we drove, I tried to think of a way of convincing her to give it up. Or at least to find someone else to do her dirty work. I drew blanks. She turned off onto a county road and parked. I parked behind her. She powered down her window, leaned out and yelled, "Get in."

I got out of my car and slid onto the passenger seat of hers. "All right. I'm here."

She studied me for a moment. "Are you wearing any kind of recording device?" she asked.

That was when I realized I was dealing with a very careful lady. First, driving out of town where there was no one to witness our meeting. Next, checking me for a tape recorder. I shook my head no, but she frisked me anyway. She handed me a pen and notepad.

"You'll need to take this down," she said.

I said, "Whoa. What makes you think I'm going along with this?"

"You're here, aren't you?" She pushed her sunglasses to the top of her head. Her steely, pale blue eyes didn't match her dumpy body. "You know I'm serious. You know that video will get you life. Let's not waste time."

I nodded weakly. The morning was still cool, but I was sweating. Dark stains were forming half circles under my arms. Black wasn't such a good choice of color after all.

"His name is Stanley Beekland." She pushed a color photo at me. "Take a good look. I can't let you keep it."

It was a head shot of a man in his fifties, balding, glasses, round face, prissy, small, mean mouth. The kind of face that doesn't see a lot of humor in life. A lot like hers, in fact.

"Your husband?"

She paused a moment, then said, "Yes."

"Why do you want him dead?" When she didn't answer, I said, "What? He beats you? Cheats on you?" Chico had tried to slap me once and never tried it again. But he had cheated on me regularly from the get-go. And he stole from me to feed his gambling habit. I guess I was looking for some way to connect with this cold bitch.

"He's a beast," she said in a low voice.

"Can't you divorce him?"

She gave me a look that told me not to go there. Money, I figured. It always boiled down to money.

She went on, as if she were reeling off a grocery list. "He's a man of routine. Leaves the house at eight thirty, gets to work by nine. He's in charge of accounts at Sutherland's Appliances. They're on Carlingwood. He drives a purple Chevy Aveo, license BCEW 882. Are you getting all this down?"

Reluctantly I started making notes.

"He's home again by five thirty, except when he works late. He's usually alone in the building at such times, but the store's always locked up after hours. The doors work on a code, so if that's when you want to do it, you'll have to find a way of getting in. I can't help you. On Fridays he always stops off at Benny's Tavern for a few beers before coming home."

I raised my eyebrows. Benny's was a serious watering hole. Judging from Stanley's photo, I wouldn't have pegged him as the type who'd hang out there.

"On Saturdays and Sundays," Marcia went on, "he cuts the grass and washes his car. In the evenings he takes a walk before bedtime because he suffers from insomnia. Have you got all that? We sleep in different bedrooms, by the way."

I interrupted the flow. "If I do this—IF—how do I know you'll keep your end of the deal? What's to prevent you from continuing to blackmail me?"

She shrugged. "Once Stanley's dead, why would I want to turn you over to the police? You'd drag me in to protect yourself. So you see, we have a common interest."

It made more sense than her asking me to trust her. Mutual survival I could believe in. All the same, it wasn't much to go on. "You'll have to give me something more," I said.

"Like what?" Her pale eyes grew narrow.

"Oh, like a signed confession. In case I'm caught."

"It's your job to make sure you're not." She glared at me.

"Something that shows this was your idea would be good." I tore off a sheet of paper from the notepad and gave it to her with the pen.

She thought about it for a minute. "All right." She scribbled something. "That good enough for you?"

She had written *I asked Gina Lopez to kill my husband.*

I shook my head, gave her another sheet of paper and dictated, "Make it 'I confess I had my husband, Stanley Beekland, murdered.' Leave my name out and date and sign it."

She wrote *I confess I had my husband murdered*. She dated it *August 11, 2010*, and signed it *M. Beekland*.

"You forgot his name," I pointed out.

"It's good enough as it is," she snapped. "How many husbands do I have?"

I shrugged. It wasn't much of a guarantee, but at least it gave me something to hit her back with. I took the paper, folded it and put it carefully away. Then I focused on the photograph, working myself up to disliking the face enough to kill the man.

I asked, "So how do you want this done?"

She looked shocked, like I'd told her a dirty joke. "That's up to you. *You're* the hit woman. But there are four conditions. First, I want to know in advance *when* and *where* you plan to do it because I'll need to make sure I have an alibi. I don't need to know *how* it's done. In fact, I don't want to know. I don't have to tell you it's very important that you cooperate with me on this. Remember, if anything backfires on me, you'll go down too. Second, I want as little contact as possible between us. Don't call me. I'll call you. You have a mobile?"

I nodded.

"Give me your number and keep it on at all times."

I wrote it down for her.

"Third," she said, "I pay you nothing. As long as I keep quiet, you'll collect on the insurance and you'll stay out of prison. That should be enough."

She really was a mean bitch. But organized. I had to give her that. "What's thc fourth condition?" I asked, trying to keep my voice calm.

That was when she dropped the bomb. "You have seven days, including today, to do it."

I stared at her, thinking I couldn't have heard right.

"Seven days?"

"Until next Sunday, to be exact. So you'd better get moving."

"Forget it," I said, opening the car door.

"And the video?" she said. "You don't expect me to forget that, do you?"

I was so whapped by her seven days I'd almost forgotten the damned video. Slowly I shut the door again, thinking if I had to knock anyone off, it should be *her*.

She must have read my mind. "There's something else," she said. "If anything should happen to me, I want you to know I've set things up so a CD of the video goes straight to the police." She smiled a nasty smile. "I'll give you until tomorrow morning to think of something. I'll call you in the morning. You'd better have a plan. Because by then you'll have only *six* days."

CHAPTER FOUR

I didn't make it in to work at all that day. I didn't even bother calling Roz. My life was going down the toilet; why did I need a job? I wound up at Al's, leaning on my elbows at the bar while Jimmy set up for the afternoon trade. The place was empty except for us. Al was out somewhere, probably sizing up lady mud wrestlers.

By now I'd already got my head around the fact that I'd have to take Stanley out. It was a matter of survival. I had Marcia and the cops coming at me from one side, Bernie the loan shark from the other. My problem was I was new to murder. Oh, I read the papers and watched the news on TV, and I knew people killed other people every day. Trouble was I had no experience. I slid off the stool to help Jimmy shift a couple of kegs. Then I went back to leaning on my elbows.

"You okay, kid?" Jimmy asked. His deeply creased face, partly covered by a fall of bleached-out hair, was worried. Like I said, he was a good friend.

"Yeah," I said.

"I talked to Al about a rematch," Jimmy said, thinking this was what was bothering me. "I'm afraid he wants to run a chick named Janey Jumps from New Liskeard against Wanda on Sunday. You heard of her?"

"No," I said dully.

"He thinks a new face will bring in more business."

"So what am I? Last night's takeout?"

"Don't be that way, Lava. He'll have you up again next month for sure."

"But I heard Wanda's moving on to Detroit after next week." I'd have given a lot to be wrestling in Detroit.

"Well, maybe you need the break. Maybe this thing you got with her is messing up your head."

"I told you—"

"Yeah, I know. She butted you. She's also got fifteen pounds on you. She's a heavy contender, Lava."

"She's fat," I said.

"It's her diet," Jimmy said. "Her standard intake's a double bacon burger with a side of super fries. You see where fast food gets you." He was a health nut, big on organics and green vitamins and always on me about the junk I ate. He punched my arm. "Hey, cheer up. I've never seen you this down before."

"Oh," I lied, "I guess I'm still getting over Chico. But I'm also sick of wrestling small-time mud. The Vegas Championships, Jimmy.

That's what I'm aiming for. I know I've got what it takes to win big."

"Sure, kid," he nodded. "I believe you." And he meant it.

Jimmy was not only my main cheering section and best friend, he was my source of good advice. His rough past was carved on his face. He'd been in and out of jail and had a history with drugs. He'd been clean for years now, but was battling diabetes, which gave him problems with his feet. Maybe because he'd seen so much of life, he was a good listener. And great at problem solving. Well, I had a problem.

So, trying to make it sound casual, I said, "Suppose you wanted to kill someone, Jimbo. How would you do it?"

He stopped wiping down the bar to frown at me. Then he grinned. "You thinking of Wanda?"

"You got it." I went along with the joke. No way could I tell him I was serious.

He shook his head. "Oh boy, this is going way beyond personal."

"Indulge me." I laughed. "Let's say I want to bump her off. How would I do it? And get away with it, of course."

He shrugged. "Bash her on the head."

I made a face. "Messy."

"Well, drive-by shootings are very popular."

"Don't own a gun."

"Drown her in Lake Ontario?"

"With all that blubber? She'd *float*."

He guffawed. "What about a knife? 'Cept with her it'd probably be a flesh wound." He didn't like Wanda any more than me.

"Look," I said, "give me something fast, easy and untraceable. And before you go there, I know zilch about poisons."

He picked up a bottle of Johnny Walker, squinted at the float line, put it down and rubbed the side of his nose. "Well, there's always an empty hypodermic."

"What good would that do if it's empty?"

"It's *because* it's empty. You stick it in a vein and shove the plunger. That pushes an air bubble in. It creates an air lock that stops everything dead. Lights out. It's called an air embolism and it looks like a heart attack."

Now he had my attention. "Would it be traceable?"

"Can you trace air?" He snapped the towel.

"I like it," I said.

"Although it wouldn't be easy," he warned. "Because you'd need to inject a lot of air. You'd need a frickin' horse syringe." Jimmy, an ex-junkie, knew a lot about needles. He also had to inject insulin every day for his diabetes. He grinned. "Don't worry. I got a vet pal who could maybe help you out. But you'd also need to find a vein. You can't just jab anywhere. Look." He extended his arm, made a fist and showed me a blue, ropy bulge in the crook of his elbow. "*That's* a vein. I don't think

Wanda's gonna hold still long enough for you to find the sweet spot."

I could see the approach had its drawbacks.

Jimmy went back to wiping down the bar. After a moment, he said, "Shit, why not just run her down?"

"Don't you always leave evidence? Paint, broken glass, stuff like that?"

"No problem if they don't have a car to match it up with. Do it so no one sees you."

"Ha! With my luck, there'd be a cop cruiser right behind me."

He sighed. "Okay. If you don't mind a spell in jail, hit her in broad daylight, at a busy intersection. Just make sure you breathalize over the limit. Drunk driving causing death is never good for more than a few years."

"No thanks. I value my freedom." I wasn't joking.

"You're hard to please, Lava." He was getting tired of the game. "Look, why not just hire a hit man? Now that's the really *smart* thing to do. Course, you'd need to pay him."

Marcia was plenty smart, I thought gloomily. And she didn't need to pay *me*.

CHAPTER FIVE

Marcia's call dragged me awake too early Tuesday morning. In the background at her end I could hear the faint beeping of a garbage truck, then the groaning of its engine as it rolled off. She was outside somewhere, using a pay phone. What did I say? Careful and smart. No way was the call going to be traced to her.

I was still groggy, and I wasn't prepared for what she tossed at me.

"Do it tonight. He's working late."

"What?" I was still trying to clear my head.

"Tonight. He'll be in the building alone. Do it then."

"Hey, whoa, you can't just expect—"

"Do you have a problem?"

"So how do I get in?" I remembered she said the place was always locked up after hours and the doors operated on a code. "Or do I knock?"

She yelled at me, "That's *your* problem! You work it out." And in a more normal voice, she said, "I have my quilting class tonight. It's the perfect alibi."

I hung up on her. Screw her and screw her alibi. That's all that mattered to her—being in the clear while I did the dirty work. I felt sick and dizzy. I slumped on the edge of the bed for a moment with my brain between my knees and my stomach in my mouth. Marcia's video kept replaying before my eyes. What I saw was not the push that she accused me of, but the moment when I didn't grab Chico to pull him back. A voice in my head said,

Are you crazy? There was no way you could have saved him. You would have gone over with him. Another voice said, *You let him go. You're exactly what Marcia says you are. A killer.*

The realization seemed to switch something on in my head. If a killer was what I was, a killer I'd be. I'd be smart and I'd be careful. And I'd get away with it. I squinted at the clock. Seven something. I went into the bathroom and threw cold water on my face. I put on shorts, a T-shirt and runners, slapped on my Ray-Bans, grabbed my iPod and my car keys and headed out.

I left my car on a side street and trotted up to Sutherland's Appliances. I was a typical jogger out for her morning run. There was no one about. The store didn't open until nine. I detoured for a little sprint around the building. Sutherland's was a big square cinderblock of a place. There were keypads at the front and side entrances. The only other way in was through a big service door at the loading bay around back. That had a keypad too. There were big show windows on the street side and a couple of little windows high up on one side of the building, where I figured the toilets were. There were red and black stickers everywhere: *Ransom Digital Security*.

I strolled down to the Tim Horton's on the corner and ordered an icing-loaded cruller and a double-double. Jimmy hated my choice of breakfast foods. The sugar hit made my stomach cramp. I called my boss and explained that my broken tooth had somehow morphed into a jaw infection. She didn't believe me. By the time I hung up, my coffee was cold.

At 8:40 I was standing behind a tree at the back of Sutherland's parking lot. At 8:50 Stanley's purple Chevy turned in and pulled into a space between two cars. The color of Welsh's grape juice, it reminded me of a boxed drink. He didn't see me as he got out, but I got my first real-life look at him.

Balding on top with a little fringe of pale hair lower down. Glasses that glinted in the sun. Small and pudgy like his wife. In fact, they could have been bookends. Even in the August heat he wore a suit and tie. He carried a briefcase and a little yellow nylon bag with a Velcro fastener. I had one like it, only mine was red. Now I knew he packed his lunch, probably ate it at his desk.

He had to walk all of twenty paces to the entrance. It was useful seeing him in motion. There are things you learn to watch for in mud wrestling. How easily does your opponent move? How good is her speed and balance? Stanley walked stiff-legged, like a duck. Not a man who was light on his feet or who could change directions fast. And he had a tobacco habit. Before he went in, he lit up a cigarette, smoked it down to the nub and ground it into the standing ashtray by the door.

Well, I'd had a look at Stanley. I didn't like him any better than his wife, but I had a hard time thinking of him as my victim. If push came to shove, I knew I could overpower him. But I still wasn't convinced I wanted to kill him. I was in a sweat to find another way out of my predicament. So my next stop was the Beekland house.

Marcia hadn't told me where she lived, but all I had to do was look in the phonebook. There was only one Beekland, on Green Street. The house was one of those old brick monsters sitting on a large lot, surrounded by a lot of trees and bushes. It stood between other big, imposing houses, facing a park. There was money on this street.

I drove past, circled around and parked down the block, out of sight of the house but where I had a view of the driveway. Around half past ten Marcia's car nosed out. I ducked down fast, hoping she wouldn't recognize my old Honda. Fortunately, she turned in the other direction. I got out of my car and strolled back toward the house.

If Marcia had downloaded the video, that probably meant she had a computer. I wondered if I could break in and steal it or at least trash the hard drive. Except, knowing Marcia, she'd have made plenty of backups. She could even have emailed the video to herself, which meant it was out there in cyberspace, waiting to be viewed. And there was that thing she said about a CD of the video going to the police if anything happened to her. I guessed it would be stored somewhere safe. I thought about taking her signed confession to the cops. That would get her off my back. But then the video would come out. She really had me up against the ropes.

There was no sign of activity at the house. To be on the safe side, I rang the bell. No answer. I tried the door. Locked. I went to the back of the house and glanced around. I heard a dog barking next door, but the shrubbery screened me pretty well from the view of nosy neighbors. I tried the downstairs windows. They were locked too, but I noticed that all the upstairs windows were open to catch the morning air. For a moment I had a fantasy of breaking in and finding something really incriminating against Marcia that I could use to get me off the hook. I knew it was a nonstarter. I wouldn't know where to look. Besides, I didn't have a ladder.

I was about to leave when suddenly I heard a wail. It was harsh, coming from the upstairs window directly above my head. It sounded like an angry baby. Could the Beeklands, at their age, have a kid? More likely a Siamese cat, I thought.

I returned to my car and drove away, thinking about Jimmy's ways of killing people. *Bash her on the head*, he'd said. I went across town to Home Hardware and bought a hammer.

CHAPTER SIX

Later that afternoon, I put on pedal pushers, a slip top and a mid-length dark brown overblouse. I wore flat shoes. tied my hair up in a scarf and put on my Ray-Bans. I wore a fanny pack. I needed my hands free. I wrapped the hammer in a towel and put it in a plastic bag. Then I went back to Sutherland's.

I got there at four thirty, thinking I'd have to hang around until five. But a sign had been rolled out in front of the store that said *August Blow-Out Sale Open Till Six!* Marcia hadn't told me that. I went in.

There were quite a few customers browsing around because of the sale. The showroom was big. There were rows of stoves and fridges. There were freezers and dishwashers. Over by washing machines and dryers, a salesman was hard-selling a couple with twins in a double stroller. A skinny guy with an earring breezed up to me.

"Right, how can I help you?" he said.

I pretended to be looking for a fridge. He said they only came in black, white and stainless. He talked about cubic capacity and the advantages of a pull-out freezer drawer. I nodded and said, "Uh-huh," but all the while my eyes were darting here and there, searching for a place to stow myself until after closing. When Stanley would be alone.

There was a sales area off to the side with chairs and a couple of desks. A gray-haired woman was sitting at one of them working at a computer. Beyond the sales area was a hallway. I told the salesman I'd think about it and walked away. I strolled past the woman and moved casually down the hall. If anyone stopped me, I'd say I was looking for the washroom. But everyone was too busy to notice. I passed doors that said *Men* and *Women* on one side of the hall and a door on the other labeled *General Manager*.

The last door down, partly open, said *Accounts*. I glanced in and saw Stanley. He was sitting at his desk, in profile to me, pecking at a keyboard. The way his head poked back and forth as he typed reminded me of a chicken. I tried to hang on to that image. Killing a chicken didn't seem so bad.

I went back to the Womens. It was like a normal bathroom, a single toilet—no stalls—and a sink. There was air freshener and hand cream on the counter. There was a pebbled-glass window high up in the wall above the toilet. I sat down on the toilet to have a think.

The way Stanley's office was set up I couldn't just sneak up behind him and hit him on the head. I'd have to take him by surprise and do it fast before he could react. I went through the whole thing step-by-step. Get hammer out. Move quietly to the door. Quick peek in to check his position. Rush him. Whack. I imagined the splatter. I expected there would be a fair amount of blood and even brains. I pushed down a feeling of pre-kill nausea. *Remember, he's a chicken*, I told myself.

When I'd done it, I'd shove his body behind the desk. They said the longer a body takes to be discovered, the less chance the cops have of catching the killer. I'd shut the door. I'd go back into the Womens—no, that's where'd I'd outsmart them—I go into the Mens. I'd clean up there. I'd take off my blood-stained overblouse, wrap the hammer in it and put them with the towel in the plastic bag. Then I'd leave. I'd dump the bag in a lake, weighted down by rocks. The rest of my clothing I'd put in different Goodwill drop boxes in another city.

My immediate problem was where to lay low until closing time. I thought about hanging out in the washroom but remembered the woman at the computer. She looked like the type who'd come in for a pee before she left.

I went back out and wandered through the showroom again. It led off into a receiving area where appliances still stood in their boxes. The back doors of the shipping bay were closed. There was no one there. I glanced behind me. All of the salesmen were too busy winding up their pitches to notice me. I found a spot to hide among the crates.

* * *

A bit after six the place began to clear. I heard people saying, "See ya," and "You in tomorrow?" and "Helluva day." After a while someone yelled, "Okay, Stan. I'm closing up." Then there was silence.

I waited, more to steel my nerve than to make sure Stanley really was alone. After a bit I slid out, crossed the showroom and the sales area, paused at the head of the hall to listen. I'd never really understood the phrase *deafening silence*, but I understood it then. My ears rang with it. It went on so long I almost convinced myself that Marcia was mistaken. Stanley wasn't working late. He'd gone out with the others. Killing him would have to wait for another day.

And then from his office I heard a sneeze. It was a little noise but it exploded like fireworks in my head. At the same time I felt like someone had kicked me in the gut. I took a couple of deep breaths. *Chicken, chicken, chicken*, I told myself. I pulled the hammer from my bag and started down the hall.

I was nearly to his door when another noise made me freeze. It was a clang, like the front entrance had just been banged opened. There were voices, whistling. Something was dropped and rolled across the floor. Someone laughed. Then I heard the whine of a vacuum. *Oh shit*, I thought. *The cleaning crew!* That was one thing I hadn't counted on.

My first thought was to duck into the Womens. My second was that they always cleaned in there. I slid into the General Manager's office. They were sure to clean there too. I wondered if I could fold myself into a filing cabinet.

I opened the General Manager's door a crack. The vacuum was still going. Then it cut out. I strained to clue in to what the cleaners were doing, but there was only that deafening silence again. Suddenly I heard a grating noise in Stanley's office, like he'd shoved his chair back and was getting up. I pushed the door shut and leaned back against it. I was like a rat in a trap, Stanley on one side, the cleaners on the other.

Calm down, calm down, I told myself. *You haven't killed anyone yet. The only thing you've done is be here after closing. There's a Plan B. Abort. Just walk out. Smile at the cleaners like you're an employee and walk out.* They *won't know. But do it* fast. *Before* he *sees you*. I peered into the hallway. It was empty.

My legs wanted to run like hell, but I forced them to carry me normally down the hall and into the sales area. From there I could see that there were two of them, a man and a woman. The man said, "Piece a junk." Both were bending over the vacuum. *Here goes*, I thought. *Make it nice and casual.*

In the next instant, footsteps behind me sent me diving for cover. I nearly choked as Stanley waddled by not more than six inches from my face. He failed to see me only because he never turned his head. I peered out from behind a desk in time to see him go out the front door. It took me a moment to pull my scrambled thoughts together. He'd gone. He'd finished his work, packed up and gone. I felt the sweet letdown of relief wash over me. *You don't have to do it*, I told myself. *You can't. Not tonight. Give him a few minutes to drive away. It's still Plan B.* Only then did I realize I still clutched the hammer in my hand. I stowed it in the bag.

By the time I decided it was safe to move, the cleaners had got the vacuum going again. I stood up cautiously. They were down at the other end of the showroom, the man pushing the vacuum, the woman walking around, emptying wastebaskets and doing a pretty spotty job of dusting. My way to the outside world was clear.

I was almost to the double glass doors when I saw something that nearly made me scream with fright. Stanley was standing just outside them, not more than five feet from me. I was down behind a fridge so fast it made me dizzy. He hadn't left! The chicken hadn't left! His back was to me and he was standing out there, scratching his stomach and having a smoke.

He walked right past me again on his way back down the hall. My mind was whirling. *Okay. Okay. He's still here. Back to Plan A. You can still do this. Just wait until the cleaners go.*

For the next hour I played a crazy game of duck and run as the cleaners moved about the building. They worked their way into the sales area. I scrambled on all fours for the cover of a bank of stoves in the showroom. The woman went down the hall with a little trolley loaded with a bucket and a mop. I stayed put. The man came back into the showroom. I scuttled behind a freezer.

I stayed there motionless so long I was beginning to feel like part of the display. Then the woman returned. The man began winding up the vacuum cord. They wheeled the vacuum and their equipment trolley to the front. I blew out a lungful of air.

At that point Stanley appeared. He had an unlit cigarette in his mouth. Smoke time again.

"All done?" he asked the cleaning pair.

"Yeah," said the man. "Took a little longer than normal. Vacuum's acting up."

"You go first," Stanley said around his cigarette. "I'll arm the system."

You go first? I peered out. He was going for a smoke, but he was *also* carrying his briefcase. This time he really was leaving. I'd just spent an hour in hell on my hands and knees and the little nerd was leaving! There was nothing I could do but crouch tight behind my Maytag. The cleaners wheeled their equipment out. Stanley punched a keypad I hadn't noticed on the wall inside the doors. I heard a beep and saw a flashing red light go on. As he killed the overhead lights and pulled the door to behind him, something locked in place inside my head. I thought, *Oh shit!*

That was the second thing I hadn't counted on. The keypad and the flashing light meant I needed a code to get *out*. I sat there so long my feet went numb. But my brain was boiling. There was only one thing I could do. Spend the night. I'd have to find a place to hide. I'd have to hope no one would find me before the store filled up with customers in the morning and I'd be able mingle with them and walk out.

I unfolded myself and stood up. That little movement was enough to blow the roof off and me with it. The lights went on, an ear-splitting shrilling filled the air. I'd triggered the motion detector alarm.

I didn't wait. I sprinted for the Womens washroom, jumped up on the toilet. The window was just big enough for me to squeeze through, but it was sealed shut.

I smashed the glass out with my hammer, cleared away the ragged shards with the hammer claw and squirmed up, over and out. I landed in a dumpster full of cardboard. I hoisted myself out of it and hit the ground face-first. I lay there for a moment, stunned. My hands and arms were cut, my nose was bleeding. Then I was up and limping off as fast as I could go, leaving the wail of approaching sirens behind me.

CHAPTER SEVEN

I was ready for Marcia's call the next morning.

"Have you read the paper?" she demanded.

I said truthfully, "No."

"The police said it was a break-in. Was that you?"

"I don't want to talk about it," I said. "Does Stanley suspect anything?"

"I don't think so. But the police do. Because a window was broken, but the glass fell *out*, not in."

"That's weird," I said.

"You have five days left."

"It's no good reminding me."

"Well, what are you going to do about it?"

I was ready for this too. I'd spent all night thinking about it. "I'll do it when he takes his walk."

"Tonight," she snapped. "Make it tonight. It's supposed to rain tomorrow."

"All right, all right. What time does he go?"

"Ten thirty, eleven."

"Does he take the same route every night?"

She took a moment to answer. "He usually goes around the park, down Green to Maitland, left on Boswell, left again on Crawford and back to Green. It takes him about half an hour."

I thought fast. "So he doesn't have to cross any streets?"

"He does if he wants cigarettes. He has to cross at Maitland and go two blocks up to Main to the Shortstop." She paused. I could hear the gears turning in her head. "I could ask him to pick up something for me."

I took a deep breath. "Okay. Do that. And call me the minute he leaves the house."

"Fine," she said. I'd given her the when and where. She didn't bother with the how. Like she said, she didn't want to know.

Out of curiosity, I asked, "So what's your alibi?"

She said coolly, "I have a cousin in British Columbia. Their time's three hours behind ours, so it won't be too late to ring her after he goes. We talk for hours. If you're quick about it, I might still be on the phone with her when the police come with the bad news."

* * *

That afternoon I got to know the geography of Green Park. It was a big rectangle of trees and grass running between four streets, just as Marcia had described. I parked my car a few blocks away and walked back. Maitland was a quiet road with houses set back from it with lots of shrubbery. That was good because it meant no one had a clear view of the road. Traffic was light even during the day—the occasional car, the odd dog walker, a few teenagers on bikes, moms with strollers. There'd be even less activity late at night.

The Maitland end of the park had lots of bushes and a floral clock. There was no stoplight at Green and Maitland, but there was a streetlamp. I picked out a spot on Maitland on the park side, about half a block west of where it crossed Green. I paced out the distance from there to the intersection.

Then I turned up Green and walked south as far as the Beekland's house. When I was even with it, I turned around. I checked my watch and timed the walk from their house back up to Maitland. I went slowly to match what I thought would be Stanley's pace. I made it in thirteen minutes.

As I walked, I tried to think of what I was doing as prep for a wrestling match. I tried to make myself focus on the moves.

Only this time it wasn't arm or leg locks, it was keeping the car idling with the lights out, judging the distance, imagining Stanley stepping off the curb, letting out the clutch and stamping on the gas. I thought I'd need to be going at least sixty to kill him, and I figured I'd hit him just as he was a third of the way into the road. I could almost feel the impact, see his body flying, all arms and legs, as I kept going.

I groped my way to a bench and sat down. It was a hot, muggy day, but that wasn't the reason I was soaked with sweat. I still couldn't believe I was actually going to murder someone.

* * *

Nightfall brought no relief from the heat and humidity, only mosquitoes. You could feel things building up to a summer storm. Rain was not predicted until tomorrow, but the way things were going, I figured it would move in early just to thwart me. I didn't park at the spot I had chosen on Maitland but instead chose a position on Boswell, north of Maitland. I got there at ten. I didn't know how long I'd have to wait for Marcia's call, and I saw no point in being too obvious.

I tried to keep my mind free, my body loose. That's hard to do when you're crouched low, white-knuckling a steering wheel.

"Oh, Chico," I moaned. "Why? I wouldn't be in this mess if you hadn't wanted a quick way to some cash. Sure, we fought over your gambling, your playing around, but life together had its good times. In the end, did I really mean so little to you?" I started crying.

The tweeting of my mobile nearly sent me through the roof.

"Yeah?" I realized I was shouting. My hands were shaking.

"He just walked out the door. He's going to the Shortstop. Get him this time." Marcia hung up.

My heart was thumping in my throat. I felt the familiar nausea. I could barely focus on my watch as I began the count. One minute. Two. Three. Four. I pictured Stanley pausing to light a cigarette. At minute seven I keyed up the ignition and moved down Boswell, turning left onto Maitland.

At minute nine I slid into place and killed the lights but kept the engine running. Ten. I thought of all the things I should have done. Like gas up. I saw myself running out of gas as I tried to make my getaway. Eleven. For the first time I seriously wondered if my 1981 car had the oomph to hit sixty in half a block. Twelve. I nearly wet myself when I saw headlights coming toward me far down Maitland to the east. They moved slowly, like a cop car on the cruise. Twelve minutes thirty seconds. Stanley should be nearly at the intersection. He'd cross and I'd slam into his body in full view of that damned oncoming motorist.

Yes, Officer, I saw the whole thing. The driver went right at him, as if she meant to run him down. Yes, I'm pretty sure it was a woman even though it was dark. And I know it was a Honda Civic, blue. I even got the last three digits of the license plate if that helps.

Thirteen. The car swept past in a quiet rush of air. Fourteen. Fifteen. At minute sixteen I heard myself screaming, "Where the hell are you?"

And there he was, moving slowly into view. I recognized his stiff-legged gait. The streetlamp gleamed on his bald head. I gunned the motor just as he stepped off the curb.

That was when I saw the dog. It was more a blur with a tail, low to the ground. Damn Marcia! She didn't tell me they had a dog. Instinctively I swerved. I expected to hear the screaming of a squashed dachshund. My momentum carried me up on the sidewalk. I swung the steering wheel to miss the streetlamp. I overcorrected and shot across the pavement. I knew I had to get out of there, so I didn't brake. Instead I accelerated.

That was my first mistake. My second was to check my rearview mirror, where I caught a glimpse of Stanley standing in the middle of the road. Then I saw the mailbox rushing at me. I swerved again and clipped wing mirrors with a parked car. I kept going, zigzagging wildly from side to side down Maitland, bouncing off the curbs on both sides, whanging garbage cans that had been left out for pickup, dodging more streetlamps and finally, crunching my right fender on a guardrail.

CHAPTER EIGHT

The tweeting of my phone woke me up on Thursday morning.

"Go 'way," I groaned. I was hungover from all the scotch I'd drunk to calm my nerves and groggy from the sleeping pill I'd taken to knock me out. I didn't want to greet the world. I didn't want to explain to my angry boss why I wasn't going to be in again that day. Most of all I didn't want to talk to Marcia.

My phone went on chirping at me. I stumbled out of bed and groped around. I found it under a pile of clothes.

"How're we doing, Mrs. Lopez?"

It wasn't Marcia. It was the broken-nosed gorilla Bernie, doing his weekly follow-up. Things were still at the polite stage.

"Nothing yet," I said.

"It's been a month. My people don't like being kept waiting for their money."

"Look, back off, will you?" I tried a weak threat. "I can take this to the cops, you know. I'm sure they'd like to know about people like you."

"Not a good idea." He didn't sound so friendly now. "Besides, it's a legit business loan. I got the paperwork and all. A wife's responsible for her husband's debts, ain't she?"

"I'll call you when I have something," I said and hung up.

I'd hardly put the phone down when it rang again.

I snatched it up and yelled, "I said back off!"

"This morning," Marcia hissed like a viper in my ear, "he was down for breakfast.

I want to know why he was eating an *egg* this morning when he *should have been dead!*"

I sank down on the edge of the bed, reliving my nightmare escape down Maitland. I remembered the air dancing with garbage cans, my car dragging metal, sparks flying. There was no way I could claim the damage on insurance.

"Why didn't you tell me about the damned dog?" I croaked. My head was pounding.

"What dog?" she screeched.

"The one he takes for walks!" I found the strength to yell back. "A little thing. Short legs. Long body—"

"You fool! That's the neighbor's dog. He wanders loose a lot. He follows everyone."

"Look," I said. "Call me back in thirty. I can't deal with this now."

I disconnected and staggered to the bathroom. I stood under a shower so cold it made my butt ache. I dried off and stared at my face in the mirror. My skin was pasty. My eyes had dark pouches like beanbags under them. *I* was the one who looked like roadkill.

I was still staring at myself when she called back.

"You now have four days," she said.

"Listen, what's your hurry anyway?" I demanded.

"That's none of your business," she snarled. "If you'd done your job right, it would be over by now. Just get on with it."

I said, "I need more information. About Stanley. He can't just go to work and take a walk at bedtime and wash his car on weekends. What else does he do?"

"He watches television."

"That's *it*?" Maybe she wanted him dead because he was so boring. "Well, what are his likes and dislikes? His weaknesses? You gotta give me something I can use."

"He's"—she lowered her voice—"he's attracted to big women." She made it sound disgusting.

"So?"

She said stiffly, "You haven't seen his magazine collection. He hides it under his bed. His favorite is *Big Fat Mamas*. He likes them oversized with big breasts. He circles their boobs with a red marker. The centerfolds, I mean."

I almost laughed. Well, well, well. Who would have thought it of Mr. Duck Walk, with his bald head and necktie and little lunch bag? An idea was forming in my mind.

"You said he stops off at Benny's on Friday nights. How long does he stay?"

"Depends. A few hours. He's usually home by ten."

I wondered if Stanley went to Benny's to pick up big fat mamas. If he did, he must have been a quick worker to be home by ten.

"Who does he drink with? People from work? Friends?"

"He has no friends. As far as I know, he drinks alone. But he never gets drunk. He doesn't hold his liquor well, so he's very careful. Are you thinking of doing it then? I need to know because—"

I cut her off. "Yeah, yeah. You need to set up your precious alibi. Let's just say he may be a long time coming home."

Before I hung up, I asked, "Did he mention anything about last night?"

"Not a word," said Marcia.

* * *

After I hung up with Marcia, I called Jimmy. He wasn't pleased to be rung out of bed at such an early hour.

"Jimbo," I said. "You know that horse syringe you mentioned? I need one. Don't ask why."

I heard him groan off-phone. He mumbled, "Hang on a minute." He put down the phone. After a while I heard a toilet flush in the background. When he was back, he said grimly, "You on drugs, kid?" He disapproved strongly of drugs now that he was clean. He knew firsthand what they could do to you.

"For cripes' sake, with a *horse* syringe?" I kept it lighthearted. "Can you ask your vet friend? I really need that needle and I need it pronto, Jimbo. It's—it's for a joke on Wanda." I hated lying to him. "Nothing bad. Just something to take her down a slot."

That put him in a better humor. "Oh, well, in that case. I'll see what I can do."

"This afternoon? Thanks. Love ya." I switched off.

I didn't bother calling Roz with more lame excuses. I banged my right front fender back in place and headed out of town. I drove to London. It was a long way to go shopping, but I knew better than to do anything locally.

My first stop was a corner store. In the magazine section I found the latest copy of *Big Fat Mamas*. Marcia was right. The feature babes were *large*. I tried to imagine Stanley with one of them and nearly choked. I drove to the east side of town to a specialty boutique called HERZ. Before I went in I put on my headscarf and sunglasses. The woman there wanted to be helpful, but I said I was just browsing. When I found what I wanted, she said, "Might I interest you in another style, ma'am? These aren't very—ah—*durable*." I just smiled.

I stopped off at a Shoppers Drug Mart for cosmetics, then a place called The Costume Bazaar where I bought a wig. The nylon hair was curly, long and red.

At the Value Village on Wellington, in women's fancy wear, I tried on a very low-cut satin dress. It was size XL, grape purple to match Stanley's Chevy, and hung on me like a sack. It was a little worn under the arms but it would do. In sports-wear I found a tired-looking, stretchy one-piece swimsuit. It was also XL and would have easily fit Jabba the Hutt. In accessories I unearthed a fake leather burgundy handbag with a silver chain. My final stop was Jake's Mill. It carried everything from remnant carpeting to knitting yarn to underwear. I bought a large, two-inch-thick foam-rubber pad.

On the drive back to Franks, I swung by Al's.

Jimmy was at the bar. He pushed something in a paper bag across to me.

"Is this a syringe or a caulking gun?" I asked, looking in the bag. It was a lot bigger than I expected.

"It's was last used on a stallion named Rondo," he chuckled. "In case Wanda asks."

"Awesome," I said.

He took a closer look at me. "What happened to you, kid? You look like hell." He gestured at my swollen nose and scratched arms and hands. He hadn't seen me since my disaster at Sutherland's.

"Fight with a dumpster. Thanks, Jimbo." I gave him a swift peck on the cheek to avoid further questions and left.

I was dead tired and my head was buzzing, but I didn't go back to my apartment and crash as I was aching to do. I went downtown to check out Benny's Tavern.

I'd been to Benny's once or twice but not recently. Since I started mud wrestling and because of Jimmy, I did my drinking at Al's. Benny's was a raunchy establishment, not unlike Al's, with hot-pink neon lighting spelling out the name over the door. In the window was a sign advertising *Friday Happy Hour 5 to 7 Drinks Half Price*. The tavern stood in what over the years had become Franks's skid row. There was a Canadian Cab office on one side of it and a takeout pizza on the other.

I didn't need to go into Benny's. I already knew the layout, a typical saloon, long bar, tables in the middle, booths at the back. But I wanted to have a look at the alley running behind the tavern. My getaway route. It was narrow and dark and smelled of garbage and cat pee. Benny's back door was propped open. Inside I glimpsed a dim hall tiled in dirty, cracked linoleum and stacked with crates of bottles and beer kegs. Farther down were the doors to the washrooms.

I hadn't eaten much all day, so I went back out to the street. A hulk in a red tank top stretched over a beer belly was having a smoke on the sidewalk in front of Benny's. At the pizza place next door I ordered a pepperoni, black olive and hot pepper takeout.

"Benny's busy on Friday night?" I asked the pimply kid working the ovens. He shrugged. "Ask Ox," and pointed a floury finger at the big guy outside. "He's the bouncer."

I decided to pass on Ox.

I took my pizza home, ate half of it and fell asleep in front of the TV. When I woke a little after nine that night, I felt so dry I drank a liter of coke. I finished off the pizza. I spent an hour on the Internet looking up veins. I spent another hour practicing finding them in my arms. Then I had a shower and crashed.

* * *

I spent most of Friday getting dressed. I measured and tried the foam on several ways. Finally I cut it crosswise into a couple of two-foot strips. I taped the strips around my middle and pulled the swimsuit over it. I stood in front of the mirror. My new look was barrel-shaped. Then I blew up the supersize inflatable push-up bra I'd bought at HERZ and put it on. I pulled the grape-colored dress on over everything. I had to do a bit of juggling to get my boobs to sit right, but in the end I achieved the desired effect. When I saw the finished product, I had a shock. With the red wig on, I looked remarkably like Wanda.

CHAPTER NINE

My phone warbled as I was putting the finishing touches on my makeup. Wanda went heavy on the false eyelashes and mascara when she wasn't wrestling, so I did too. She liked lipstick. I made up a bright red mouth. It's not that I was consciously setting out to frame her for murder. I just needed a big woman to model my new self on, and she seemed to fit.

"What?" I barked, expecting it to be Marcia. I was feeling as strung out as a high-tension wire.

"Yo, Lava." It was Jimmy. "When are you gonna do it?"

"Do it?" I squeaked. How the hell had he found out what I was really up to?

"Wanda," he said. "The big joke."

"Oh. Right." I peeled myself off the ceiling. "Tell you about it later."

At five o'clock I was ready. I slipped the hypodermic in the burgundy handbag, breathed deep and went for my car. I cruised slowly past Benny's. Stanley's Chevy was nowhere in sight. People were drifting into the tavern for the happy hour. Mostly a young crowd, guys in jeans and muscle shirts, chicks in shorts and halter tops. A few in working clothes. I circled the block and kept circling until luck finally broke my way. A 4x4 pulled out of a slot just opposite the tavern entrance. I managed to slide in ahead of another car and got a loud horn for my trouble.

It was another sweltering night. The promised storm that was supposed to break the heat hadn't arrived. To make things worse, I was wearing a wig and four inches of foam. I was sweating like a pig and I felt my makeup sliding. My car didn't have air conditioning. I tried fanning myself with a road map folded into quarters. It came apart at Kitchener-Waterloo. I was sinking into a soggy mess by the time the purple Chevy finally showed. It did the routine drive-by, looking for a parking spot. Eventually it headed up the street to the pay lot on Boxwood.

Here we go, I told myself as I watched Stanley return on foot and push through the tavern door.

I allowed him half an hour before I followed him in. The bouncer Ox gave me the once-over as I entered. Up close I saw that his belly actually masked a lot of muscle.

"Hey, big girl." He looked amused. He'd changed from his tank top to a T-shirt that said *Benny's*, and he'd slicked his black hair straight back. "You come equipped with a forklift or what?"

For the first time in my life I was aware of the shit fat women have to put up with.

"No, I use a trolley," I said, playing the good-natured, oversized broad, but I thought, *Dick-head*. I gave him a wink, felt my false eyelashes stick together and quickly headed for the bar. I pried my eyes open and checked out the crowd. At least the place was air-conditioned. I pushed my elbows out to air my armpits. A smartass behind me said, "Awk, puk puk puk." I knew I ought to go to the Womens to repair my makeup, but at that moment I picked out Stanley perched on a stool, staring into a beer. I pushed in beside him and jogged his elbow just as he was raising his glass.

"Hey!" he objected.

"Oh, I'm so sorry," I said and made a show of mopping up his sleeve.

"Well, you ought to be more careful." He had good reason to be annoyed. I'd really made a mess. But as he sized me up, his scowl faded. His eyes swirled toward my cleavage like water down a drain.

"Another beer for the gentleman, and the same for me," I told the bartender, who grinned. And to Stanley I said, leaning in, giving him an even closer view of the falls, "That was terribly careless of me. I really do apologize."

"Oh, that's all right," he breathed, looking kind of stunned. I doubted he'd ever been picked up before. He didn't seem to know the moves.

Our beers came. The person sitting next to Stanley left and I claimed the stool, sliding my bottom on it in a way he wouldn't miss. He couldn't even if he'd wanted to. In my foam padding, I took up most of the view.

"I hope you don't think I'm being forward," I said. "But I'm new to town and I'm finding it kind of lonely. Folks here are nice enough but a bit standoffish, don't you think?"

"What? What?" he babbled. He recovered. "I mean, what's your name?"

"Wa—" I broke off. I couldn't do it to Wanda. "Washington."

"Washington?" He looked puzzled. "Isn't that a state?"

"It's my last name."

He laughed, a kind of haw-haw. "Oh. Like George Washington."

"Except my name's Sally."

"Oh. Sally Washington. Well, mine's Randy."

"Randy?" That brought me up short. Had I been targeting the wrong victim?

"Randy's what I get when I meet a lovely lady like you, haw-haw." His left hand went for a wander over my bum while his right hand set his glasses straight. I changed my mind about him. He knew the moves all right.

"Oh, you!" I gave him a playful sock that rocked him back. I hoped I'd left a bruise. "No, seriously, what's your name?"

"Stan," he said, trying to make it sound manly. He whispered hoarsely in my ear, "Has anyone ever told you, your breasts are like two big bouncy balloons?"

I wished I'd brought my hammer. *The night is young*, I told myself and gulped my beer instead. The hand was back. This time I let it stay.

By nine the Happy Hour customers had cleared, leaving the hard-core drinking crowd. I'd been plying Stanley steadily with beers. He let me do the buying. At the rate he was downing them, I figured I should be charging Marcia expenses. The upside was that the barman and the bouncer Ox would remember that Stanley's last hours were spent in the company of a heavy-set redhead with a triple-D cup, not lean, trim Gina Lopez.

By now I had a pretty good idea of what I was up against. A suppressed drunk, a closet letch. Everything about him was so buttoned-down but wanting to come out, he was bursting like a sausage. His eyes were the same pale color as Marcia's. He breathed annoyingly through his mouth. He had a disgusting leer. He was in his own heaven with me, a seriously large lady. At least he'd go out smiling. Out of the corner of my eye, I spotted an empty booth.

"Look." I swiveled his stool around so hard he almost flew off it. "Why don't we go back there?" And I called out to the bartender, "Two more of the same."

I carried our drinks. He followed me across the room, rolling unsteadily from side to side.

"You first," I said, pushing him in ahead of me. I had to help him scoot along the bench. I slid in next to him on the same side. We were wedged tighter than sardines.

"Why don't you get comfortable, take your jacket off, dude?" I gave him an inviting smile and twisted around as far as my foam allowed to give him a full view of the goods on display.

"Comf'able as I am," he giggled, but he didn't resist when I stripped him of his outer layer. I was relieved to see he wore a short-sleeved shirt. It would make my job a lot easier.

"You told me you're an accountant," I said sweetly.

"Yeah. A calculator cowboy." More haw-haws.

"Well, I just think that's wonderful because I happen to be looking for an accountant."

"Y'are?" He squinted at me. He pulled free of my grip, put his hand on the inside of my thigh and pinched so hard I nearly screamed. I pried his fingers loose, slapped his hand back on the table and pinned his arm in place.

"Y'r eyes..." he burbled, "are like runny poo—poo—pools."

And yours, I thought, *are like two mashed grapes. You got a mean streak in you, pal. No wonder Marcia wants you dead.*

"Stan-boy," I simpered, "I got some tax forms I just can't figure out. I'd give a lot to have someone like you look at them."

"Loo—lookin' at 'em now." He hiccupped and tipped sideways. His nose was almost down my dress. He collapsed heavily against me, snoring in my cleavage.

Dream on, I thought. I had the needle in my right hand, plunger at the ready. With my left I stroked his arm, pushing and prodding for a vein. I located something stringy inside the hollow of his elbow, just below the surface of his skin.

Die happy, jerk, I thought, and jabbed him. Or I tried to. But he sat up just as the needle descended and it speared the table instead.

"Ooh, look," he burbled, pulling it out. "A hypo—hypo—hermic." He waved it around. "Lez play doctors and nurses."

I tried to snatch it from him, but he was as slippery as a fish. With a cross-eyed ogle, he grabbed my boob and stabbed me with the needle.

It should have hurt, but I felt nothing. Only a weird, sinking sensation as the push-up deflated with a hiss, leaving my left breast going south. Stanley watched in fascination.

"You got one tit higher'n th'other," he mumbled in a puzzled voice. "Hey!" he yelled, like he'd been cheated. "How come you got one ti—"

I clamped a hand over his mouth and snatched the needle from him. Ox was moving our way.

"Everything cool here?" the bouncer asked.

"Yeah," I said. "We're just having fun."

"No, 'm not," shouted Stanley for everyone to hear. "Sh—she's got 'neven tits." He poked my lopsided bustline hard, making it squeak and sag some more to Florida.

Ox broke into a grin as he eyed me.

"It was just a joke," I said.

"Lemme out." Stanley was really mad. He pushed and punched me off the bench. Ox let it happen.

"I'm goin' home." Stanley staggered a step or two before Ox caught him on his way down.

"You're going in a cab, man," said Ox.

"I'll take him," I said, standing up. "I'm fine to drive." If I couldn't do the job at Benny's, I'd do it in my car and dump him somewhere out of town. At that point I really did want to kill him.

Ox looked me up and down. His mouth was stretched wide, ear to ear. "No way, lady. You've had a skinful too. I'm calling *you* a cab."

I knew when I was beaten. "Okay, big guy." I gave him a heavy flutter that sent one of my fake eyelashes sailing. "But first I have to visit the little Ladies."

The bouncer was now laughing so hard I had to shove him out of the way. I waddled across the room to the whistles of the hard-core drinkers, through the swinging door with the hand pointing *Toilets This Way*. I went past the Womens, past the kegs and crates of bottles, out the rear exit and kept going.

CHAPTER TEN

Marcia yelling at me on the phone first thing in the morning was getting to be a bad routine. I hated her uppity, nagging voice. I hated her telling me I'd failed again. I hated her saying I now had until tomorrow to do the job. I hated *her*. But when she *didn't* call first thing Saturday morning, I began to get nervous. I found myself talking to her in my head, making excuses. I'd given it my all. It wasn't my fault her horrible husband was still alive. Whereas *my* life was all but over. Come Monday I'd be looking through bars.

People went missing every day. I decided I was going to be one of them. I had a few hundred in the bank, a credit card not yet maxed out and a banged-up car. Enough to get me—where? Winnipeg? Calgary? Vancouver? I'd run. I'd go underground. I'd get away from the mess my life had become.

I told myself, *Okay, girl, stay cool. You've got a lot to do*. I drove downtown and closed my checking account. I stopped off at a pharmacy and came back with a box of Clairol and a bottle of Liquid Bronze. I took a pair of scissors and hacked my hair off real short. A few hours later, I was no longer blond with shoulder-length hair but darkest mahogany, gelled up into spikes, and my skin was a few tones darker. I looked like a giant hedgehog with a tan. I wasn't crazy about my new appearance, but I had to say even my own mother wouldn't have known me.

I packed only the clothes I needed, some camping gear, my iPod and my mobile.

I boxed up the food I figured I could use on the road. I tossed all my personal stuff—letters, cards, photos. I hesitated over my wedding album. It was the only reminder of Chico that I had. I decided he wasn't worth it, and it went too. I left everything else. I loaded up my car. Before I said goodbye to my apartment, I watered my plants. Maybe some kind soul would rescue them. And I called Jimmy.

"Hey, Lava," he sang out when he heard my voice. "I was about to give you a bell."

"Listen, Jimmy—" I started, but he cut me off.

"I got great news for you, kid. You got your match! Janey Jumps pulled out. You're on with Wanda Sunday."

I was so geared up for flight, I didn't know what he was talking about for a minute. My life as a mud wrestler seemed a million years ago. I dropped into a chair. At that moment I wanted to tell him everything.

About Chico, Bernie, blackmailing Marcia, Slippery Stanley and the horrible hand fate had dealt me. I wanted to bawl my head off. Instead I said, "Oh."

"Well, don't say thank-you. I had to lean on Al for this. You said it was what you wanted."

"I mean it's really great, Jimbo." I tried to pump enthusiasm into my voice.

"So, you up for this? You can win this, girl. Just get your head around it. You can win this." Good old Jimmy. Always in my corner. Always pulling for me.

Something—my backbone—stiffened. I stood up. "You're right," I said, really meaning it. "I can win this. I'll flatten the head-butting bitch. And thanks, Jimbo. Thanks a lot."

I unloaded my car and humped my stuff back up to my apartment. I could run another day. I thought, *Damn Marcia*. And then I called her.

* * *

"I told you not to contact me," she barked as soon as she recognized my voice. "I was going to call you—"

"Shut up and listen," I told her. "I'm not doing your dirty work. You want him dead, you do it. And you can take your video and shove it."

"Hold on. Not so fast. You still have time..."

She went on talking, but I shouted over her, "You deaf? I said no. Nix. Niente. You're finished using me."

"...it's simple, foolproof, and this time I'm even going to help you."

"What?" I said.

"Domestic accidents happen all the time. Stanley's away for the afternoon. So the coast is clear for you to booby-trap the cellar stairs. Think about it, Gina. It's him or you. Is he worth a lifetime in jail?"

He wasn't. She'd called him a beast. I knew he was a sadist. I didn't feel sorry for her being married to him. She got what she deserved. But *I* deserved better than a permanent berth in prison for a death I did *not* cause, even if I had to commit murder to make sure that didn't happen. I knew now I couldn't have saved Chico. I hadn't *let* him fall. He'd set up his own exit, and there was nothing I could have done about it.

Her plan was simple. Stanley always watched TV on Saturday nights. His favorite show came on at 8:00—*Creeps*, a new thriller series. I thought the name suited him. All I had to do was rig a wire across the cellar steps and trip the circuit breaker sometime after 8:00. The wiring in the house was old. Fuses were always blowing. The fuse box was in the cellar. Stanley would grab a flashlight and go down to the cellar to the get the power up again. Marcia would make sure the flashlight had dead batteries. She'd already arranged her alibi. She was going out. And Stanley would go bump.

Her plan was simple, and it was smart. As I listened to her talk, I really began to think I could have it all. I could get rid of Stanley, get Marcia off my back and drag Wild Woman Wanda through the mud.

CHAPTER ELEVEN

Marcia had told me to come around to the rear of the house because she didn't want the neighbors to see her letting me in. She was waiting for me at the back door and jerked it open before I could knock.

"Who—?" she started to say until she realized it was me in my new look. If she suspected I'd been preparing to cut and run, she didn't say. Just, "Did you bring everything you need? I can't be expected to supply anything. Nothing must link—"

"I know," I sneered, "to you." The fact the murder was going to happen in her own home didn't seem to count. As long as she was out of it. "Yeah, I got the stuff." I had bought wire and nails from Home Hardware. I already had the hammer.

She got right down to business. "The cellar stairs are off the kitchen." She led the way in through a mudroom and a pantry. The kitchen was roomy and old-fashioned, with a worn tile floor and painted cupboards reaching to the ceiling. But the appliances were new and gleaming white. It figured.

She pointed to a door at the far end and said in her hoity-toity twang, "I'll leave you to it." She stalked off, very lady-of-the-manor. I was the hired help. Except I wasn't being paid.

I opened the cellar door and groped for a light switch. A single bulb dangling from the ceiling gave weak lighting to some very steep, narrow, wooden stairs. I went down them carefully, surprised no one had broken their neck on them before now. They ended in a real cellar, not a basement rec room. It had an earth floor, something you don't see except in old houses. The fuse box was on the wall near the bottom of the stairs. There was a lot of dusty, cobwebby junk piled up all over the place. The air smelled damp and moldy.

I chose the third step down. It wasn't rocket science, two nails and a bit of wire strung tightly across the side supports. The job was done in five minutes. Then I realized there were two problems. First, I wasn't supposed to trip the breaker until after eight o'clock. But if Stanley came down the stairs for any reason *before* then, he'd turn the light on and he'd go down carefully, like I did. A wire across any of the steps would be visible. I'd have to do something about the lightbulb. Second, I had forgotten to bring a wire cutter.

"Marcia?" I called.

No response. I went up into the kitchen and called again. I wandered through the dining room into the living room. Everything in the Beekland house was like a freeze-frame from an old movie. The furniture was heavy mahogany and overstuffed upholstery. The oak floors were highly polished with dark carpets here and there. Heavy curtains blocked out the sun. Gloomy paintings hung on the walls. There were knickknacks and framed photos everywhere. Gents in jackets and women in hats and mid-length dresses. There was a studio shot of a boy and a girl that I figured were the Beekland's kids when they were little. They were both chubby and blond and had a discontented look that had stayed with them in later photos that I saw. I knew why, growing up with such parents.

That was when I heard the wail. It was high-pitched—the same sound I'd heard when I'd prowled around the house four days ago, only weaker. It came from upstairs, and this time I knew it wasn't a cat.

I wondered again if the Beekland's had a kid, but it sounded more like a soul in distress than a baby. Something funny was going on. All along I'd been praying for a way out. Maybe—just *maybe*—this was something I could use against Marcia to even the playing field.

The big oak staircase was uncarpeted. I took the steps quietly. There was an open door just off the landing. I looked in. I saw a sunny room and something I had totally *not* expected—an old woman propped up against some pillows in a bed. Her eyes were closed. She was thin, with white hair, and her arms and face were covered in bruises. She'd been eating something and food had spilled down her front. When she tried to raise a hand to pick at her soiled nightgown, I saw that she was strapped into the bed.

"What are you doing here?"

I whirled around. Marcia was standing right behind me. She looked furious.

"I'd like to know what's going on," I demanded. From her startled expression, I thought I had her. This helpless, battered old woman, tied down against her will, was something Marcia didn't want the world to know about. And my ticket to freedom.

The woman's mouth twisted open, and another cry filled the air. Up close it grated on my nerves.

"Get out." Marcia shoved me away from the doorway.

"Who is she?" I said, holding my ground in the hall.

"My mother," Marcia snapped. She carried a wet towel in one hand, a squeeze bottle in the other.

"Your m-mother?" I stammered.

"Yes, my mother," Marcia said impatiently.

"Why's she tied up like that, if she's your mother?"

"She's ill. She tries to get out of bed and falls down because her balance is bad.

She hurts herself, so she has to be restrained. Now if you don't mind, I have to clean her up. Have you finished?" She jerked her head, meaning downstairs.

"Need a wire cutter," I mumbled, backing away.

"You were *supposed* to bring everything with you." She was madder at my failure to come equipped than at my discovery of her mother. "There's a toolbox in the cellar. You may find something there."

I did. Marcia came looking for me just as I was finishing up.

"I'll have to loosen the lightbulb," I warned. "In case he comes down before eight."

"He won't, but better to play it safe. Just don't forget to tighten it again. And dismantle the wire. After."

Her mind really did work like that.

"Be here by seven thirty," she barked out orders, timing it to the minute. "The coal door to the cellar at the side of the house will be unlocked. Let yourself in and wait. I'll go out at seven fifty. His program comes on at eight o'clock. I'll leave the door to the kitchen open so you can hear the TV. Pull the circuit breaker just when the action's building up. Best to do it after eight fifteen and before eight forty-five, but not during a commercial. My neighbor across the street is home tonight and I told her I'd drop by to make a Heart and Stroke contribution. She collects for them. I'll stay there chatting until I see the lights go out here. I'll make sure she notices too."

Her foolproof alibi, I thought.

"Which reminds me," she went on. "The cellar windows are curtained, but use a penlight, not a flashlight, just in case. I'll get him good and mad before I go. That'll put him in the right frame of mind. I want him stewing and in a hurry. He'll storm down the steps, and goodbye Stanley. Oh, one last thing. Make sure he's dead.

If the fall doesn't kill him, you'll have to finish him off."

"Any suggestions how?" I asked, laying on the sarcasm. "I can't exactly stab or shoot him if he's supposed to die in a domestic accident."

She gave me a pitying look. "*You're* the wrestler. Break his neck."

She'd worked it out, down to the last detail. I knew her plan would succeed, and I knew why all of mine had failed. I was not a natural killer. Marcia was.

CHAPTER TWELVE

I was back at the Beekland house by seven thirty. The coal door wasn't like a normal door. It opened up out from the ground into a chute. It was where coal for heating used to be dumped in the old days. It was still daylight outside, but as I slid down the chute into the Beekland's cellar, I slid down into darkness. But not silence. Marcia had promised a fight, and there was a humdinger of a shouting match going on upstairs. I sat at the bottom of the chute for a moment, listening. I couldn't make out words, just angry voices. They were really going at it. *Maybe they'll kill each other off,* I thought. I'll be rid of both of them. I'll just slip away the way I came. After dismantling the wire and tightening the lightbulb, of course.

I flicked my penlight on and followed the narrow beam to the foot of the cellar steps. As I crept up them, I checked the wire. It was in place, so tight it plinked. Good to her word, Marcia had left the door leading into the kitchen open a crack, letting through a sliver of light. I switched off the penlight and sat on the top step. From there I could hear more plainly.

"Cheap, cheap, cheap!" Marcia was yelling. "Too cheap to send her to a nursing home. To cheap to hire a nurse."

"And you're too effing lazy to take care of her," Stanley yelled back.

"Oh sure, it's fine for you. You go out to work. I'm stuck with all the cleaning up."

"You know she wants to be cared for at home. And she doesn't want a nurse. What Mother wants Mother gets. Don't forget that."

Marcia said in a sneery voice, "Oh, you're the golden boy. But don't think she doesn't see through you. She's never trusted you. Even when you were a snotty kid. You were sneaky and mean then. You're sneaky and mean now. She's always known what you're like."

Stanley laughed. "And you think she hasn't always known what a little brat bitch you are?"

"You make me sick!" Marcia wasn't faking it. She really was in a fury. "I'm going out!" And then there was a scuffling and a bump, as if she'd shoved Stanley out of the way, and the front door slammed.

Golden boy? Snotty kid? Little brat bitch? I was getting whiplash from trying to wrap my head around what I'd just heard. I recalled the way Marcia had hesitated when I'd asked her if Stanley was her husband.

I'd been too rattled at the time to check if she wore a wedding ring. I remembered that I thought the two of them looked like bookends. And then I had it. The photographs I'd seen weren't the Beekland's kids. They were the *Beeklands*. Stanley wasn't Marcia's husband. He was her *brother*.

I'd jumped to the conclusion, but why had she gone along with the lie that he was her husband? To bring me on board, because she thought I'd killed mine? To throw me off the scent of what was really going on? What *was* really going on? One thing I knew for sure. She was a smart liar who was probably laughing her head off at this moment. Her so-called written confession that she'd had "her husband" murdered wasn't worth a damn since she didn't have one. I remembered how she'd refused to name him, and she'd probably disguised her handwriting. I had to face up to the fact that Marcia had run circles around me from the start.

The blare of music startled me. Stanley had turned on the TV. I fought down the same old pre-kill nausea. It didn't really matter if they were Siamese twins, I told myself. Marcia had the video, and I had a job to do.

Bang-on eight o'clock, the theme song of *Creeps* came on, and then an ad for Nissan. I heard Stanley walk across the kitchen. I heard the fridge door open, the hiss of a pull-top, cupboards banging, the crinkle of plastic wrap and him walking back into the living room. Marcia was wrong about one thing. Their argument hadn't put him in a rage. He was calmly settling down to watch his favorite show with a beer and chips.

The way a TV thriller works is this: they hook you straight off to get you into it. Then there's a commercial break. Then more action. As the tension mounts, the commercials get more and more frequent because by now they know you're not going to switch to another channel. You want to know how it ends.

I only had the sound track to go by, but I could tell when a commercial came on. I knew when the program resumed by the rise and fall of voices, and I could figure out the action from the music. I knew whenever it got low and scary—sort of *dunh dunh dunh dunh*—building up to the screech of violins, something bad was about to happen. I timed it to perfection. Right on 8:23, just as the music hit a breaking point, I pulled the breaker.

The thin wedge of light at the top of the stairs went out. The music stopped. I didn't hear Stanley yell, "Shit!" as I'd expected. There was only silence. As if he was just sitting there. Across the street, Marcia would be at the neighbors, watching the Beekland house go dark. Finally, I heard him get up and move across the floor above my head. I pictured him looking for a flashlight, discovering that the batteries were dead. He took a very long time doing it. Now I heard a bump, like he'd knocked into the furniture, then footsteps and the sound of something being dragged around. The door at the top of the staircase creaked open. A pause. My heart skidded in my throat. Suddenly, like a nightmare, something large and formless came hurtling out of the darkness at me. I jumped aside and felt the rush of air as it sailed past. It hit the lower part of the stairs once, bounced off and landed beyond me with a sickening thump.

* * *

Nothing happened. Nothing moved. It's done, I thought, it's over. Judging from the absolute stillness, I knew I wouldn't have to finish him off. At that moment, I couldn't say what I felt. Relief? Or more an awful emptiness, like I wanted to curl up on the dirt floor of the cellar and die myself. Or cry. This was no Laurel and Hardy act in a home appliance store no crazy bumper-car ride, down a city street, no disastrous comedy impersonation in a sleazy saloon. This was real death. This was murder. And I was now a bona fide killer. I knew that nothing would ever be the same.

I took a gulp of air and switched on my penlight. The first thing I saw was his arm. It was twisted under his body in an unnatural way. When my beam traveled along his shoulder to his chin, I saw with surprise that something had been stuffed into his mouth. His pale eyes were wide open and strangely naked. He'd lost his glasses on the way down. Then I had a shock. The *hair*. The hair was wrong. There was too much of it! In a panic I brought the penlight close to shine it fully on the face. It wasn't Stanley. It was Marcia.

A flickering at the top of the stairs made me look up. He was standing there, in the doorway, a candle in one hand, what looked like a gun in the other. I stood up slowly, then bolted for the coal chute, but he called out, "I think you'd better stay."

I stopped and turned. Stanley pointed with the gun. "Is she dead?"

I nodded. I didn't need to check. There was no life in those staring eyes.

"I heard her go out!" I screamed at him.

He laughed, a really nasty sound. "You heard the front door slam. But she didn't leave. She couldn't."

"What did...? It was supposed—"

"To be me? Give me some credit. I knew she was up to something. I mean, the car that nearly ran me down? And that was you at Benny's with the needle, wasn't it?" He sniggered and came down a step. The candle flame lit up his face in a ghastly way as he peered at me. "You've lost weight and your hair is different. What's your real name, by the way? Not Sally Washington, I presume?"

"Sally will do," I mumbled.

"Well, Sally, do you think I'm stupid? *Twice* in one week?"

Three with Sutherland's, I told him in my head, *only you don't know it. Four if you count tonight.*

"Why?" I cried out. "Why do you hate each other so much?"

He shrugged. "A bad case of sibling rivalry? We're twins, you see. I know twins are supposed to be close, but she was a bitch to share space with even in the womb."

Yeah. I could see Marcia planting her foot in Stanley's face in her race to get out first.

"Any more questions?" He was toying with me, and he sounded like he was enjoying himself.

I obliged. I wanted to keep him talking. "She said it had to be done by Sunday. What was her hurry?"

"Money." He breathed in through his mouth. "Our mother's very rich. She's having a brain tumor removed on Monday. At her age it's high-risk surgery. If she dies, she'll leave a couple of million behind. Marcia wanted to be sure there was only one heir. Me, as it turns out."

He looked at me curiously. "How did she recruit you? I don't suppose you're in the yellow pages."

I didn't want to answer that. Instead, I said, "How did you know it would be tonight?"

He shrugged. "Well, I was sure Marcia would have another go, and it had to be before Monday. Of course, I didn't know what or how. You might say I was in the *dark*, haw-haw." He took another step down.

One more. I held my breath. *One more and it really will be lights-out for you. Come on, you little shit.*

"Until I found the wire." He pointed to the third step. "So when she tried to leave the house, I knocked her out, tied her up and gagged her. And I waited. To see when it would happen and how you were involved. When the power went, I knew."

They were obviously twins. His mind worked just like Marcia's.

"And you threw her down the stairs?"

"It's what the two of you had in store for me."

I couldn't argue with that. "What are you going to do now?" I croaked.

"Well, let's see. If you don't tell, I won't." He actually giggled. "In a minute I'm going to call nine-one-one." He held up the gun. That was when I saw it was a mobile phone. "But first you'd better untie her and get rid of the gag. Got to make it look natural. Get rid of this wire too. Then you're going to say we were all upstairs watching television. You're my alibi, you see. A friend of Marcia's. She invited you over. The lights went out, and she had a bad accident."

I didn't wait to hear more. This was *his* murder, not mine. Let *him* make it look natural. I wasn't hanging around to alibi him. I scrambled up the coal chute, out of the cellar and ran. I was pretty sure Stanley would stick to his accident story. He had to, but either way I didn't care. I didn't care that my prints were on everything, the wire cutter, the lightbulb, the steps. I'd been so sure of Marcia's plan I hadn't bothered with gloves. I didn't care that Stanley might one day discover Marcia's video or my real name. I just wanted to be out of there, out of the house, away from the horrible Beeklands.

* * *

On Sunday night, Wild Woman Wanda really ground my face into the mud. My heart just wasn't in it.

CHAPTER THIRTEEN

Almost two years have passed and a lot has happened. Marcia's death went down as an accident. I never had any follow-up from Stanley. I didn't exactly hang around waiting for him to follow up. The day after my defeat to Wanda, I phoned Roz to say I was quitting my job at the post office. I loaded up my car again—I was mostly packed anyway. I left the rest of my stuff with Jimmy or gave it to Goodwill, had my mail forwarded to his address and drove out of Franks forever.

After a couple of months, I let Jimmy know where I was newly settled. I never told him about the Beeklands, about my week in hell, but I did make him promise not to tell anyone how to find me, especially not a creepy, mouth-breathing accountant or a goon with a broken nose. I laid low, ate junk food, drank more wine than was good for me and grew my hair back. Sometimes I went jogging, not for fitness but because it was a way of running out on life. As I ran, I wondered how things could go so wrong. Mostly I sat around doing nothing.

I could afford to. I was a wealthy woman. North American Life paid up, and my new bank account was richer by a quarter of a million bucks. Or two hundred and twenty thousand, after I'd settled Chico's gambling debts. Because Bernie went after Jimmy when he couldn't find me, and even though Jimmy told me to sit tight, I couldn't let them work on him.

But it was my experience with Marcia and Stanley that had really shaken me.

It left me jumpy. It left me paranoid. If life had taught me one thing, it was that I couldn't trust anyone. Monsters like the Beeklands lurked around every corner. Worse, I couldn't trust myself. I hadn't actually killed Marcia, but I'd made four attempts at murder and let myself be used by her. What kind of monster did that make me?

Then one day when I was fast approaching bottom, my doorbell rang. I'd paid off Bernie's people, so he was off my back. I figured it had to be the cops. They'd opened an investigation on Marcia's death, Stanley had cooked up some convincing story to frame me and they'd tracked me down. I got up, feeling like my body was filled with wet cement. In a funny way, I was relieved. It would be good to have it over with.

"Yo, Lava!" It was Jimmy. He came through my door like a blast of clean air.

"You're not lookin' good, kid," he said as he dumped his duffel bag on the floor. He said he'd had enough of Al and the pit. He said Bernie gave him a pain in the ass. He said he'd decided to put Franks behind him too.

Over the next few months he gave me a lot of grief about my diet and my drinking, made me start working out seriously and began lining me up for mud-wrestling matches.

I got back into things faster than I expected. I started feeling better physically. My self-confidence returned and with it, gradually, my self-respect. I regained my old fighting spirit, my desire to win. I did some promo bouts in Windsor and Toronto. I wrestled Detroit. I did tag-team events in Florida. In California and Chicago I perfected what has now become my victory dance.

Al's pit and the Beeklands are now a distant memory. My reputation and my purses have grown along with my string of wins. Jimbo and I are a couple now, not in the way you might think. He's with me on the road as my manager, cheering section, fitness trainer and life advisor. Lady Lava now gets top billing. I don't have to beg for matches. Jimbo's grooming me for the Vegas championships.

Tonight, July 10, I'm opening a new pit in Vancouver called Slurry's. It's a big venue with a huge purse because this is the premiere match. I go on in forty minutes. Jimmy's with me in my dressing room, fussing like a mother hen. He's worried on two counts. The date. It's the second anniversary of Chico's death. And my opponent. I'm up against—you got it—Wild Woman Wanda. I haven't wrestled her since Al's. She's done well, too, with a string of wins almost as impressive as mine.

"How's your head, kid?" Jimmy says.

"My head's good," I tell him. I'm fit, a couple of years older and lots smarter. I've left Chico behind me and I'm up for Wanda. "I'm going to wipe the pit with her," I say.

"That's my Lava," Jimmy croons. We trade high fives.

The crowd at Slurry's is yelling, "Mud! Mud! Mud!" as Wanda and I come out onto the floor. The emcee wears a tux and bowtie over a pair of black Spandex shorts. He introduces me and Wanda and tells the cheering crowd that the winner of this match will wrestle a mystery celeb later in the evening, free drinks for the first person to guess who. Someone yells, "Madonna?" Someone else says, "The Pope?"

Wanda makes a point of not looking at me, like I'm not worth the trouble. I use the time to check her out though. She still wears her trademark Tarzan suit, and although she's maybe gained a pound or two, she looks strong and even tougher than I remember. Her hair has gone from bottle-red to purple.

The yelling is deafening as we step into our corners. The ring is big, eight by eight, and the mud is the color of milk chocolate, clean and good quality. I can tell immediately by the smooth consistency. We do the mud bath ritual. We go into our kneeling crouch. The starting whistle shrieks.

The old Wanda would have contacted immediately. Instead, she circles on her hands and knees, inviting me to come to her. I circle too. The crowd is urging us on. We make a few tentative grabs. Someone yells, "C'mon, ladies. Let's see some dirt!" I choose that moment to launch myself at her. We slap and grapple. I'm on top and planning to stay there. I straddle her, grab her wrists, go straight in for the pin, but she bridges expertly and throws me off. I roll and scramble to my knees. She hurls herself at me.

We grapple again and roll. The mud is extra slippery and I'm having trouble holding her. She takes me by surprise by pivoting swiftly. She clamps my torso with her legs. It's a powerful hold, and now she has me on my back. I'm stuck. I kick and twist, trying to build up enough momentum to rock her loose but can't break her death grip. I know the clock is running out, because I can hear Jimmy yelling somewhere to my left. I give a last tremendous heave and wriggle free. The bell sounds.

Jimmy's there at ringside, tossing me a towel. "That was close, Lava," he says. "Watch the leg clamp. She's strong."

"She's like a python," I gasp.

The whistle blows for Round Two. This time Wanda doesn't hesitate. She flies at me out of her crouch. The impact is terrific, but I'm prepared for it. We scramble, pushing with our legs and shoulders. She lands on me sideways and goes with me as I skid across the ring. Now she's on my back, loading on her full body weight, forcing me facedown in the mud. She does her old trick of really mashing me in it. It's up my nostrils and in my eyes.

"You haven't learned much, Lava," Wanda cackles in my ear. *Oh yeah?* I think. My mouth is too full of mud to say it. I throw my head back and crack her nose. She grunts.

This buys me the split second I need to squirm free. She scrambles after me, but I swivel around and get one arm around her neck, try to lock her in a cradle. She's too experienced, sees it coming, knows it's my favorite move, and kicks loose. More scrambling.

Now we're head-to-head, arms interlocked, walking in circles on our knees, pushing hard against each other. This is where her weight is always an advantage. She has a lot more to push with. I feel her draw her head back, see her eyes, know she's mad as heck about her nose. I slam my forearm into her throat.

"You try to butt me again, I'll break your neck," I spit into her face as the bell rings.

The ref has to pull us apart. I lean aside to towel off and rinse my mouth. Out of the corner of my eye, I catch Wanda staring hard at me. Her face is so covered in mud I can hardly make out her features. She's the color of a Hershey bar all over, purple hair included. I know I look the same. I don't like to think what's going through her mind.

The whistle goes.

We're both so exhausted we're happy to buy time, circling on our knees. But we know the fans want action. We crash together with a wet slap. We grapple for maybe fifteen seconds, head-to-head again, until we topple sideways. I grab her around the middle. She's as slippery as an eel. She breaks out, pivoting fast to come behind me. Her hands clasp together around my neck in what might pass as a chin lock but is an illegal choke hold. She has me tight against her and is really putting pressure on my airway.

That's her objective. I try to drive my chin down, claw to pry her loose.

She's strong, and by this time I'm seriously needing oxygen. The more I struggle, the more she has me gasping like a landed fish. The ref sees me fading but does nothing because the crowd is loving it. Before my mind goes dark, I remember an August night two years ago when she had me on the wall. I do the only thing I can to break her grip. I put up one last big show of resistance, pulling away and dragging her behind me, then suddenly give way. It's only for a second, but the feint is enough to unbalance her. I duck my head fast and roll forward, putting everything I have into flipping her right over me. She goes with my momentum, lands on her back with a satisfying splat that sends mud flying. Now I'm swarming all over *her*, putting my full weight into sinking the bitch. The crowd is going crazy. I hear Jimmy shouting, "Go, go, go for it, Lava!"

"NIGHT NIGHT, HIPPO!" I roar in Wanda's face. I get the pin just as the bell clangs.

* * *

My victory dance says it all. I pump my arms and circle my fists. I twirl and stomp and punch the air and kick. The fans love it. They're yelling and whistling and throwing twenty-dollar bills like confetti. The management keeps things at fever pitch by blasting the theme music from *Rocky*.

The emcee shouts a lot of hype about Slurry's and the celebrity match that'll be coming up later that night. Meantime, hit the bar, friends. Jimmy throws a towel over me. I do a final victory pirouette and head to the showers. No hosing down outside first, like at Al's. The crowd applauds me as I go. On the way, a man pushes through to catch my attention. He's short and bald with glasses. At first

I don't recognize him. And then I do. It's Stanley. "Outta the way, pal," says Jimmy. "The lady's got to take her beauty bath."

"We're old friends," says Stanley, trailing me all the way to the dressing room door. I see he's lost a lot of weight, but he's still a mouth-breather and a little shit.

"Hey," says Jimmy. "Get lost."

"She'll want to talk to me," says Stanley. "I found something that belongs to her."

An old fear falls over me, heavier and colder than a mudslide. "It's okay, Jimbo," I manage to say. "I know him."

Jimmy gives me a doubtful look, senses something's wrong. "You sure, kid?" He backs off slowly down the hall.

"*What*?" I whirl on Stanley, putting into it the venom of a spitting cobra.

He fakes a deeply hurt look. "Is that a way to greet an old acquaintance? I have a proposition I'm sure will interest you. You see, mother's operation was successful.

She's a tough old bird. Taking a lot longer to die than I expected. I need cash. And I found Marcia's video and all the news cuttings she saved about your husband's death. So is it Sally Washington or Gina Lopez, or do you just go by Lady Lava now?" He grins. It's more a leer. "She was blackmailing you, wasn't she? That's why you had to kill her."

My brain reels. I feel like Wanda's slammed me in the gut. "*I* had to kill her?" I croak. "It was *you*! *You're* the one who threw her down the stairs."

He shakes his head. "Not how the cops will see it. Not when they see the evidence against you. Now, I wonder if I can persuade you to do another spot of murder?"

MICHELLE WAN was born in China and grew up in India and the United States. She is the author of the orchid-themed *Death in the Dordogne* murder mystery series set in southwestern France: *Deadly Slipper, The Orchid Shroud, A Twist Of Orchids* and *Kill For An Orchid*. She and her husband Tim live in Guelph, Ontario. Visit www.orchidsaremurder.com for more information.